The Vice President of the
United States
**AR PTS
1.0
AR RL
7.5
64821**

America's Leaders

The

VICE PRESIDENT
of the United States

by Scott Ingram

BLACKBIRCH®
PRESS

THOMSON

GALE

San Diego • Detroit • New York • San Francisco • Cleveland • New Haven, Conn. • Waterville, Maine • London • Munich

For more information, contact
The Gale Group, Inc.
27500 Drake Rd.
Farmington Hills, MI 48331-3535
Or you can visit our Internet site at http://www.gale.com

LIBRARY OF CONGRESS CATALOGING-IN-PUBLICATION DATA

Ingram, Scott (William Scott)
  The Vice President of the United States / by Scott Ingram.
    p. cm. — (America's leaders series)
Includes index.
Summary: Discusses the selection and duties of the The Vice President of the United States, where he works, his daily routine, responsibilities, chain of command, and what a typical day might be like for the Vice-President.
  ISBN 1-56711-662-0 (lib. bdg. : alk. paper)
  1. Vice-Presidents—United States—Juvenile literature. [1. Vice-Presidents.] I. Title. II. Series.
  JK609.5 .I54 2003
  352.23'9'0973—dc21

                                                                2002008418

Table of Contents

A Changing Position

More than 200 years ago, a group of men wrote a document, the U.S. Constitution, which established the American government. The authors of the Constitution divided the government into 3 separate branches, the legislative branch, the judicial branch, and the executive branch.

Under the Constitution, the legislative branch was made up of the Senate and the House of Representatives. The judicial branch was the nation's court system, with the Supreme Court as the highest court. The third branch of government, the executive branch, was led by the president.

The Constitution established the position of vice president as part of the executive branch. It states: "In the case of the removal of the President from office, or of his death, resignation or inability to discharge the powers and duties of the said office, the same shall devolve upon the Vice President as part of the executive branch."

The U.S. Constitution established our nation's government.

In his role as president of the Senate, Vice President Lyndon Johnson sat on the left behind President John F. Kennedy during Kennedy's State of the Union address in 1962.

Part of the vice president's responsibilities also fall under the legislative branch. The Constitution states: "The Vice President of the United States shall be President of the Senate, but shall have no Vote, unless they be equally divided."

Few positions in the U.S. government have changed as much over the past 200 years as that of the vice president. At one time, the position was almost totally ignored. The vice president did not even regularly attend the president's important meetings until the 1930s. As the U.S. government grew at the end of the 20th century, the vice president took on a wider range of responsibilities. For some presidents, the vice president became one of the most trusted advisers.

> **USA Fact**
>
> In 2002, the annual salary of the vice president was $186,300. The vice president is also allowed $10,000 for personal expenses. The annual salary of the first vice president, John Adams, was $5,000.

A Job of Sudden Importance

Few Americans paid attention to the position of vice president until 1841. In April of that year, one month after his inauguration, William Henry Harrison became the first president to die in office. Vice President John Tyler suddenly became the president.

Tyler's move up to the presidency led to important questions. Was he the acting president or the actual president? Would he serve out Harrison's term, or should a new election be held? Tyler declared that he was the actual president, and he went on to serve out Harrison's term.

In 1841, John Tyler became the first vice president to assume the office of president.

Vice President Lyndon Johnson was sworn in as president aboard Air Force One *after the assassination of President John F. Kennedy on November 22, 1963. Kennedy's widow, Jacqueline, is on the right.*

Seven times during the next 125 years, a vice president assumed the presidency. In each case, no vice president was appointed to take the vacant position. From 1841 until 1967, the vice president's position was vacant for a total of 37 years.

By 2001, the vice president had become one of the most important people in the executive branch. Today, the vice president is a member of the president's advisory group, called the cabinet. The vice president may help the president choose other cabinet members. He or she is also a member of the National Security Council, the president's advisory group on international matters. Since the middle of the twentieth century, presidents have asked vice presidents to lead committees on national issues such as the space program, government efficiency, foreign relations, and national energy programs.

Vice President Lyndon B. Johnson meets with President John F. Kennedy in the Oval Office.

Vice President Al Gore (third from left) attends the dedication of a military memorial.

The vice president's main responsibility is to help the president carry out his job. The vice president may meet with leaders in the United States or abroad in place of the president. The president may send the vice president to the Capitol to convince Congress to pass or defeat certain bills. The president often asks the vice president to help raise money for their political party's candidates. Finally, the vice president may attend important ceremonies or visit places in the United States where natural disasters have occurred.

Helping the Vice President Help the President

Because the executive branch is the largest branch of the U.S. government, presidents have always turned to others for help in making decisions. Since the time of George Washington, the president has worked with a group of advisers called the cabinet. The vice president is the only member of the president's cabinet who is elected.

As the vice president's job has grown in importance, he has turned to assistants and advisers who help him do his job. The chief of staff is the vice president's most important adviser. He or she keeps track of appointments and committee meetings and sets the vice president's schedule.

Other advisers meet with the vice president regularly. They make suggestions about assignments and projects.

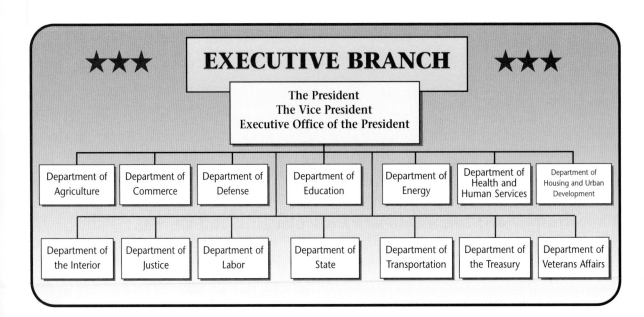

★★★ **EXECUTIVE BRANCH** ★★★

The President
The Vice President
Executive Office of the President

Department of Agriculture	Department of Commerce	Department of Defense	Department of Education	Department of Energy	Department of Health and Human Services	Department of Housing and Urban Development

Department of the Interior	Department of Justice	Department of Labor	Department of State	Department of Transportation	Department of the Treasury	Department of Veterans Affairs

President Ronald Reagan and Vice President George Bush meet with an adviser to discuss a drought affecting several states.

The vice president depends on these people to inform him about issues such as national security, energy policies, and economic matters. That way, he can make decisions that support the president's goals.

Today, the vice president often appears on news discussion shows or in interviews. For these appearances, he needs people to help him communicate a point of view that agrees with the president's. The director of communications and the press secretary help the vice president prepare for media appearances. They also handle day-to-day announcements and news releases that come from the vice president's office.

The vice president also speaks at various times to the American people as well as to the media. He may use a speechwriter to help him put his ideas into words.

Where Does the Vice President Work?

The vice president's office is in the West Wing of the White House, close to the president's Oval Office. As a cabinet member, the vice president attends weekly meetings in the cabinet meeting room of the West Wing.

In addition to the White House, the vice president and his staff work in a group of offices located in the Eisenhower Executive Office Building. This building is near the West Wing on the grounds of the White House. There, the vice president works in the Vice President's Ceremonial Office. This office is used for special meetings and for press conferences.

The vice president also has an office in the Capitol. The vice president uses this office when he serves as president of the Senate or when he speaks to members of Congress about legislative matters.

The Vice President's Ceremonial Office is in the Eisenhower Executive Office Building on the grounds of the White House.

Air Force Two *is used by the vice president and other cabinet members.*

Air Force Two

To do his job, the vice president must often fly across the United States or to other countries. He travels on a special jet used by cabinet members and leaders of Congress. When the vice president travels in the plane, it is known as *Air Force Two*. Like *Air Force One*, the president's jet, the plane has been designed to carry important national leaders. The aircraft is a Boeing 757-200, which normally carries as many as 150 passengers. *Air Force Two* has a crew of 16 and carries about 45 people.

Air Force Two has a communications center, a galley, a lavatory, and 10 seats. There is also a private room for the vice president with a dressing area, a private lavatory, an entertainment system, 2 seats, and a couch that folds out to a bed. Behind the private room is a section with a conference room. The rear section has seating for 32 people, a kitchen, and 2 lavatories.

Air Force Two has more than 25 telephone lines, as well as satellite connections, televisions, and modern office equipment. It can fly nearly 6,000 miles before refueling.

Who Can Become Vice President?

According to the Constitution, a person who wants to be president or vice president must be:

• a natural-born citizen of the United States.

• at least 35 years old.

• a resident of the United States for at least 14 years.

A natural-born citizen is a child born to American citizens anywhere in the world. A child of illegal immigrants who is born in the United States is a citizen, and thus eligible to be vice president. An immigrant who becomes a citizen is not eligible.

Women as well as men may run for vice president. In 1944, Ara A. Albaugh of the Socialist Laborers Party

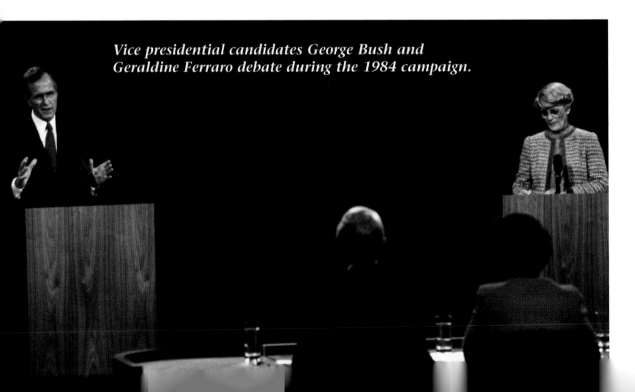

Vice presidential candidates George Bush and Geraldine Ferraro debate during the 1984 campaign.

Geraldine Ferraro, from New York, was the first woman vice presidential candidate of a major party.

became the first woman to run for vice president. Since then, 21 women have been candidates for vice president.

In 1952, Charlotte Bass of the Progressive Party became the first African American woman to become a vice presidential candidate. In 1984, Geraldine Ferraro became the first woman vice presidential candidate of a major political party. She was the Democratic nominee who ran with presidential candidate Walter Mondale. In 2000, Winona La Duke was the vice presidential candidate of the Green Party, which nominated Ralph Nader for president. La Duke is the first woman of Native American, African American, and Jewish descent to run for the vice presidency.

USA FACT

George Bush is the only 20th century president to be elected immediately after finishing an entire vice presidential term.

Running for Vice President

Many candidates for the office of vice president actually set out to run for the presidency. In 1980, for example, both Ronald Reagan and George Bush ran for the Republican presidential nomination in state primaries.

Vice presidential candidate Dan Quayle prepares to speak at the 1988 Republican National Convention.

When Bush withdrew as a presidential candidate, Reagan chose him as a vice presidential running mate.

In most cases today, the nominee for president chooses his running mate before his party's national convention opens. The vice presidential candidate gives an acceptance speech on the next to last night of the convention. From that point on, a vice presidential candidate runs against candidates of other political parties.

Election Day is the first Tuesday after the first Monday in November. In the weeks before that day, candidates for president and vice president give hundreds of speeches, shake thousands of hands, and spend millions of dollars on political ads.

They often hold televised debates with other party's candidates or have televised meetings with citizens.

On Election Day, voters cast their ballots for the candidates of their choice—the popular vote. Those votes, however, do not decide who wins the election. That decision is made by the electoral college.

To create the electoral college, the legislature of each state chooses a number of electors that is equal to the total number of federal senators and representatives of that state.

By law, presidential and vice presidential candidates who win a state's popular vote win all of that state's electoral votes. The electors of each state meet in the state's capital in December to cast their ballots. The candidates who receive the most electoral votes win the election.

The election winners are known as the president-elect and vice president–elect until they are officially sworn in.

Campaign buttons often list the presidential and vice presidential candidates.

Taking Office

For more than a century, March 4 was the traditional date of Inauguration Day. Not all Americans, however, felt that tradition was fair. It meant that the man who was leaving office remained president for 4 months after an election. In 1933, the Constitution was changed by the 20th Amendment, which set the date of Inauguration Day as January 20.

Nelson Rockefeller takes the oath of office as vice president in 1974.

Today, the vice president–elect takes the oath of office shortly before the president is inaugurated. This usually happens in front of the Capitol building on the same platform as the president. The person administering the oath may be the outgoing vice president, a member of Congress, or a justice of the Supreme Court. The vice president–elect places his left hand on a Bible, raises his right hand, and repeats this oath:

Crowds fill the area in front of the Capitol building's reviewing stand at the inauguration of George Bush in 1988.

I do solemnly swear (or affirm) that I will faithfully execute the office of Vice President of the United States, and will to the best of my ability, preserve, protect, and defend the Constitution of the United States.

President Richard Nixon (left), and Vice President Spiro Agnew (right), smile during their 1969 inauguration.

Right: An inaugural parade passes the reviewing stand during the inauguration of John F. Kennedy in 1961.

Until 1933, the vice president gave an inaugural address after taking the oath of office. When the inaugural ceremonies for both president and vice president were combined, however, the vice president's inaugural address was replaced by one address from the president. The official events are followed by a day of celebration. On January 21, the vice president takes office.

A Time of Crisis

In the election of 1800, the nation's plan for filling the position of vice president led the United States into a time of crisis. The 2 main candidates for president that year were Thomas Jefferson of Virginia and Aaron Burr of New York. The popular vote in the election was overwhelmingly in favor of Jefferson. Burr, however, carried New York and other heavily populated northern states, which gave him many electoral votes.

When the electoral college voted in December 1800, Burr and Jefferson each received 73 votes. By law, this meant that the election was sent to the House of Representatives to be decided. The winner would be president and the runner-up would be vice president.

The voting in the House went on for several months. Vote after vote was taken with no winner. Burr's most bitter enemy was Alexander Hamilton, the first secretary of the treasury. Hamilton used all of his influence to convince lawmakers to vote for Jefferson.

The election dragged on until Jefferson won in the 36th vote. Burr then became the vice president. Burr's effort to win cost him a great deal of political

Aaron Burr (right) killed Alexander Hamilton in a duel while Burr was the vice president.

power. Jefferson refused to include his vice president in any important governmental decisions. Burr became so bitter at Hamilton that he killed Hamilton in a duel in 1804. Burr became the only vice president ever indicted for murder.

After the confusion of the 1800 election, the 12th Amendment was added to the Constitution. From the election of 1804 on, voters and electors have cast separate votes for president and vice president.

Another Time of Crisis

In 1968, Spiro Agnew was elected vice president on the Republican ticket with running mate Richard Nixon.

Spiro Agnew appeared at a news conference shortly before he resigned in 1973.

The 2 men won reelection by a huge majority in 1972. Shortly after that victory, Nixon's reelection committee was linked to a break-in at the headquarters of the Democratic Party. The possibility of Nixon being removed from office was considered highly likely. If that happened, the vice president would take office.

Agnew, however, was also under investigation. In August 1973, federal law enforcement officials began to investigate him for not paying income taxes. For a while, it appeared that both the president and vice president could be removed from office.

President Richard M. Nixon met with Gerald Ford after Nixon nominated Ford to replace Agnew.

Agnew eventually reached an agreement with legal officials. He would resign from office and plead guilty to one charge instead of going to trial. While Nixon remained under investigation, the vice president resigned.

The 25th Amendment, passed in 1967, required that the vacancy in the vice president's office be filled. Nixon appointed Gerald Ford, and Ford was approved by Congress.

When Nixon resigned less than a year after Agnew, Ford became president. He was the only man ever to hold the office of vice president and president without being elected to either one.

A Vice President's Day

The day of a modern vice president is much busier than it was during the 19th and early 20th centuries. Here is what a schedule might be like for a vice president today.

Vice President Dick Cheney meets Secretary of State Colin Powell for a one-on-one discussion.

6:00 AM	Wake; shower; watch television news
7:00 AM	Driven to West Wing office; meet with chief of staff to preview calendar
7:30 AM	Meet in Oval Office with president to discuss upcoming trip to Middle East
9:15 AM	Photo session and brief question-and-answer session with new astronauts selected for space program
9:30 AM	Daily meeting with national affairs adviser
10:00 AM	Cabinet meeting
12:00 PM	Meeting adjourns; one-on-one discussion with secretary of state regarding Middle East trip
1:00 PM	Working lunch with executives regarding energy program
2:30 PM	Press conference

3:30 PM Meeting with speechwriter and chief of staff to assemble important points for evening talk show appearance

Vice President Al Gore meets with Congressman Newt Gingrich and other congressional representatives.

4:00 PM Phone call to the secretary of defense regarding budget item

4:30 PM Meeting with congressional representatives to discuss budget cuts

5:15 PM Handle pressing paperwork

6:00 PM Return to vice presidential residence; watch evening news

7:30 PM Leave for local television studio to prepare for appearance

8:00 PM Talk show appearance, answer call-in questions from viewers

10:30 PM Return to family quarters; read briefings of new developments in Middle East

11:30 PM Bed

Fascinating Facts

In 1865, Vice President **Andrew Johnson** gave his Inaugural Address after consuming several alcoholic drinks. The following day, some newspapers reported that Johnson had been drunk during his speech. Rumors of a drinking problem followed him for the rest of his political career.

Charles Curtis

Charles Curtis, vice president under Herbert Hoover from 1929 to 1933, was the only vice president of Native American descent.

Spiro Agnew was the only 20th century vice president to resign from office, and the second vice president to be charged with crimes in office.

Franklin Roosevelt had 3 vice presidents during his 4 terms in office. They were **John Nance Garner**, **Henry Wallace**, and **Harry Truman**.

At 71 years old, **Alben Barkley**, who became vice president in 1949, was the oldest person to hold the position.

Spiro Agnew

Three vice presidents were born on August 27: **Hannibal Hamlin** in 1809, **Charles Dawes** in 1865, and **Lyndon Johnson** in 1908.

John Breckinridge was the youngest person to serve as vice president. He took the office at the age of 36.

After the election of 2000 was settled by the Supreme Court, the president of the Senate opened and certified all electoral votes—a responsibility given to the sitting vice president. In 2000, that position was held by Vice President **Al Gore**, the loser in the election to George W. Bush. Gore thus certified his own loss.

Al Gore

Richard Cheney served as a defense secretary under one president—George Bush—and vice president under George Bush's son—George W. Bush.

Richard Cheney

Glossary

adviser—a person who works closely with a person in power and provides information and suggestions

Air Force Two—a jet built especially for cabinet members and leaders of Congress that houses a conference room, kitchen, and living quarters for the vice president

cabinet—a council of presidential advisers

candidate—a potential winner of an elected office

Congress—the legislative branch of government, composed of the Senate and the House of Representatives

Constitution—the document that established the U.S. government and that contains the principles and laws of the nation

Election Day—the first Tuesday after the first Monday in November on which voters cast their ballots for political candidates

electoral college—the system of electing the U.S. president and vice president in which electors from each state vote for the candidate who has won the popular vote in their state

inauguration—the act of admitting an elected official such as the president into office

National Security Council—a special section of the executive branch that advises the president on matters of national security and foreign policy

nominee—a person named to fill a certain position such as the secretary of state

oath of office—an official statement made by an elected or confirmed nominee that promises to uphold the responsibilities of office

primaries—contests in which a party's national candidate for president is elected by the members of that party

For More Information

Publications

Debnam, Wendy. *A Kid's Guide to the White House.* Kansas City, MO: Andrews McMeel Publishing. 1997.

Pious, Richard M. *Presidency of the United States: A Student Companion.* New York: Oxford University Children's Books, 2002.

Web sites

Inside the Vice President's Office

http://www.whitehouse.gov/vicepresident

The official site from the White House including the biography and speeches of the current vice president as well as a history of the office.

U.S. Vice Presidents

http://www.sittingbull.org/hallofusa/usvicepresidents

A comprehensive listing of America's vice presidents complete with biographies and historical information.

Vice Presidents Trivia Quiz

http://www.catsdogs.com/veepquiz.html

Test your knowledge of the office of vice president and all those who have served in it.

Index